Backpacks and Bookmarks

Ten Stories about School

Edited by

Frédéric Houssin and cédric Ramadier

Harry N. Abrams, Inc., Publishers

Translated from the French by Alexandra Bonfante–Warren

Design Coordinator, English–language edition: Barbara Sturman

Library of Congress Cataloging–in–Publication Data

Backpacks and bookmarks : ten stories about school / edited by
Frédéric Houssin and Cédric Ramadier.
p. cm.
Summary: A collection of ten stories expressing the ups and downs of
school days, including "Leon the Leopard Goes to School," "On the
Way to School," and "Today in the Lunchroom They Had . . ."
ISBN 0-8109-4480-4
1. Schools—Juvenile fiction. 2. Children's stories, French.
[1. Schools—Fiction. 2. Short stories.] Houssin, Frédéric. II. Ramadier,
Cédric.

PZ5. S347 2000
[Fic]—dc21   *601960826*   99-462334

Printed and bound in Belgium

Harry N. Abrams, Inc.
100 Fifth Avenue
New York, N.Y. 10011
www.abramsbooks.com

Contents

The Time-Out Box

by Christian Aubrun

Every morning, little Johnny has to travel several miles to get to school. He lives in the country. and he does not like going to school.

To meet his school friends, Johnny rides his beautiful Schwinn (that is the brand name of his bicycle).

On the way, he passes a shack where two wild cats live.

School

5

Johnny loves to talk to his
cat friends. When he gives them
little treats from his bookbag,
the kittens purr in delight.
They love the time they get
to spend with
Johnny!

"What a beautiful day"

Uh oh! Time flies.
As usual, Johnny is late for school.
He is scared of his teacher,
  Mr. Bighair, who is sure to blow
his top when he sees how
      late Johnny is.

When Johnny is late (as he usually is) Mr. Bighair grabs him by the ear and places him in the corner, in the Time-Out box.

But as he always does, good-natured Johnny just laughs to himself and thinks about the next day, when he can go see his two kitty friends.

The cats will tell him silly things about his teacher and point out that when you look at Mr. Bighair's big nose, you can see little hairs on the sides. He looks like a **big mouse!**

And that is the image Johnny keeps inside his head when he is inside the Time-Out box.

The end

Zach-Zorro

by Mireille Vautier

*Recess is Zach-Zorro's favorite part of the day.
That is when he can run and shout.*

"Charge!" Zach-Zorro cries.
He attacks Billy the Bandit
and saves Julie.

But Zach-Zorro always overdoes it,

and recess ends in bruises.

Zach-Zorro has to pay the price.
He has to sit after school as still as a mouse.

But by tomorrow, you'll see, Zach-the-Lion
will be good as can be!

End

Leon the Leopard
Goes to School

18

27.475062

Another great story from Uncle Oubrerie

It was 8:27
when Leon the Leopard
left his house.

That gave him
only three minutes
to get to school
before the bell rang.

But Leon was not worried,
because leopards
run very fast
(much faster than tortoises!).

Hey, the 8:27 stork is late this morning!

Leon is running as fast as he can and is not letting himself...

Just a quick hello to my pal Hal

Hurry!

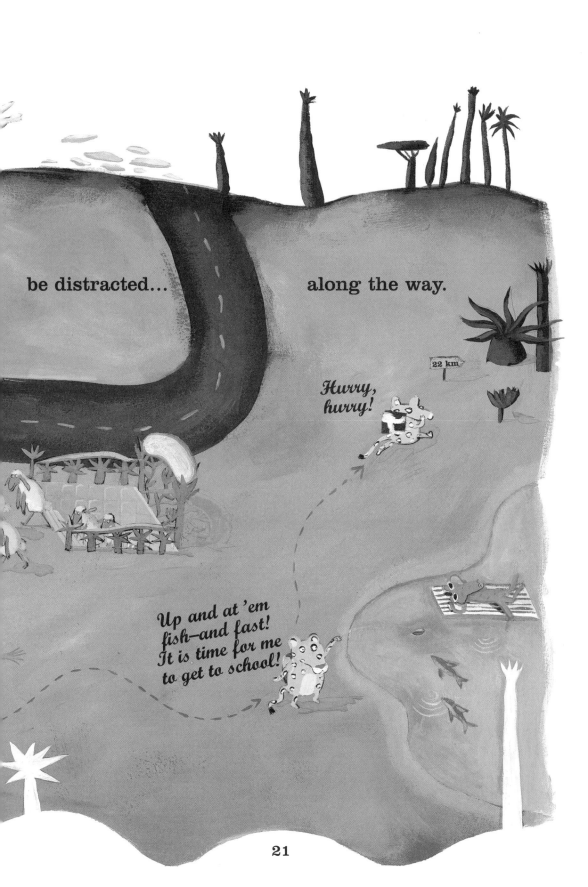

be distracted...   along the way.

Hurry,
hurry!

22 km

Up and at 'em
fish—and fast!
It is time for me
to get to school!

Like all Leopards, Leon is very skilled:

He can run...

in reverse

He can hop...

on one foot...

And on his hands...

Leon decides it is best
to run normally
the rest of the way.

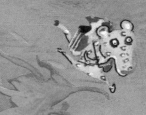

(Leon ran so fast
that he reached
the schoolhouse
before the bell!)

He rushed straight...

Frozen
Foods

to school.

Let's not
dawdle!

Eight-thirty on the button!
Leon is so proud that
he got there just in time...

for gym class!

The End

Vincent Bourgeau
Mrs. Smith's Class

Assignment: Draw and tell
a story.

The Fence

The playground
at school has a fence
all around it.

You're not
allowed outside
the fence!

Fooey! That's too bad,
because that's just what my friend
and I wanted to do—go see what's
on the other side...

Let's go anyway.
There must be some way
to get around the fence!

So we walked
for a very long time.
"Maybe the fence
never ends!"

We were just about to give up
and turn back when
a train pulled up.

31

The conductor was very nice
and he agreed to take us beyond the fence.
But suddenly, a hole appeared...

and we fell into it!
Luckily there was a ladder
so that we could climb back up.

Wow! We're so high up!
You can't see a thing in this cloud.
Let's hold on to the railing!

The railing took us back
to school. The teacher did not believe us
when we told her that we went outside
the fence!

the end

READY, SET, SCHOOL!

BY FABRICE TURRIER

back to school

It is time to pack your bookbag. What do you think should go inside?

a triangle?

a fish bone?

a pair of scissors?

an airplane?

glue?

COLLE

an alarm clock?

roller skates?

sunglasses?

pencils?

a glass?

a ruler

a diving mask?

a notebook?

thermos?

a spoon?

a frog?

a slingshot?

an eraser?

a bow tie?

soap?

a toothbrush?

a wheelbarrow?

a teddy bear?

felt markers?

Locate all these characters on the left-hand page and look at them carefully.

What is Alexa doing? ❶

What is Terry doing? ❷

What is Paul doing? ❸

What is Nancy doing? ❺

What is Harold doing? ❹

What is Max doing? ❼

What is Luke doing? ❻

What is Sophia doing? ❽

What is Arthur doing? ❾

What is Alex doing? ❿

What is Quentin doing? ⓫

What is Eric doing? ⓬

❶ Alexa is carrying a box of felt markers ❷ Terry is making paper cutouts ❸ Paul is reading his favorite book ❹ Harold made a sock puppet ❺ Nancy is playing dominoes ❻ Luke is picking up his eraser ❼ Max is making a rocket out of modeling clay ❽ Sophia is writing ❾ Arthur is proud of the shoe he drew ❿ Alex is drawing a car ⓫ Quentin is sticking paper fish on his back ❸❾ ⓬ Eric is looking for his ruler in his bookbag.

the lunchroom

One small mistake and oops! lunch is all over the table!
But who knocked over the spaghetti?

Find the clumsy one from the clues given:

Count the children starting at the bottom
of page 40. The culprit is the eighth, the one looking away!

1 How many girls are there?

2 How many boys are there?

3 How many braids are there?

4 How many striped shirts are there?

5 How many balls are there?

6 How many pairs of glasses are there?

7 How many hoops are there?

8 How many books are there?

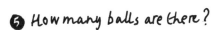

9 How many false noses with moustaches are there?

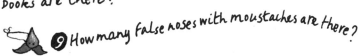

10 How many caps are there?

① ten ② twenty ③ three ④ six ⑤ five ⑥ four ⑦ seven ⑧ two ⑨ one ⑩ four

the end

Bird School

by Serge Bloch

At school, the baby birds are learning to fly.
When the weather turns cold,
they will say bye-bye.
All except Romeo, who is very afraid.
He thinks they are up too high.

At school, the baby birds are learning
to catch their dinner.
All except Romeo,
who is very picky.
He thinks worms are way too icky.

At school, the baby birds
are learning to talk.
All except Romeo,
who does not
utter a squawk.

47

Then one day, winter arrives.
The baby birds fly off,
as they have been told to do.
All except Romeo,
who was left hungry and cold, too.

It snowed so much,
Romeo was invisible.
Poor bird, he was miserable.
Would this be the end
of our scared little friend?

No, Romeo decided.
I will not just die.
I will have to learn to fly!

Romeo ran in the snow.
He ran and he ran until

he did it, he flew off
and you could hear him
in the sky so blue
CAWing! and CHIRPing!
and CHEEPing! too!

the end

Agnès Rosse
On the Way to School

Where I live,
in northwest Paris,
is where
France looks up.

(But I always look down.)

Because the way
from home to school...

is a straight line,
always,
that's the rule.

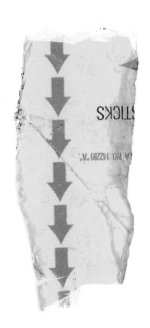

down, I still stop a lot.

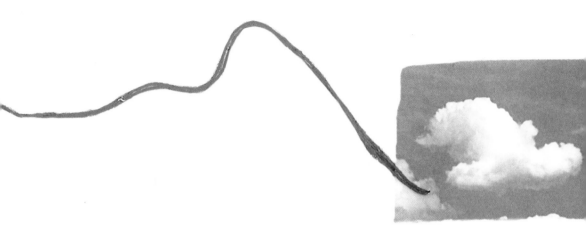

In the morning,
on the way to school,
my thoughts
are scattered everywhere.

On my way, I can make a straight turn…

to the right,
to pick up
a can
of tomatoes…

to the left,
cut here, done.
Mission accomplished.

Wow,
up high, a butterfly
flying faster
than the subway…

Over there,
a little feather.

What weather!
Even the price
tags are free!

   I make castles in my mind, and I turn to find…

I have added
incorrectly.

I might say,
so to speak,
that there is a peak
on my way…

Paths
stuck
to bottles…

and, depending on the tide
(and the street sweepers),
seaweed that has never seen
the sea and plant food
for my plastic flowers.

Okay, just 3 or 4 pieces.

And if I run into

the neighbor I most often meet

I slip him into my front pocket,
all coat-cosy.

I think that sometimes it would be good
(not on purpose of course)
to forget to go to school.

Then suddenly I realize

that I am very late.

I rush
to my seat
where
I must
always
look
straight ahead.

the end

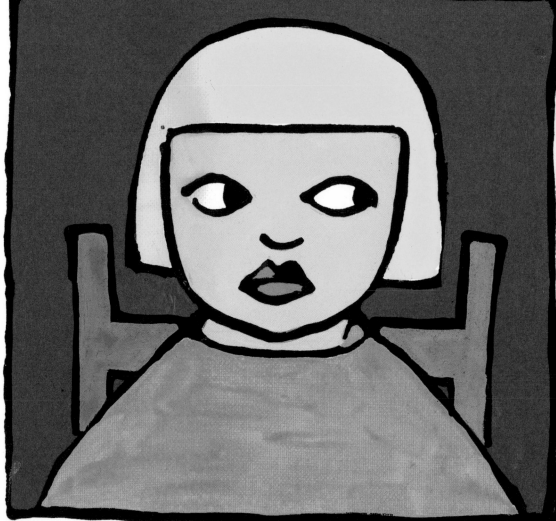

TODAY IN THE LUNCHROOM THEY HAD...

by Bénédicte Guettier

I WRAPPED THE FISH IN A PAPER NAPKIN AND PUT IT IN MY POCKET.

THERE WERE WORMS IN THE CHERR "IT'S JUST MEAT!" SAID THE LUNCH LADY. **UGH!**

64

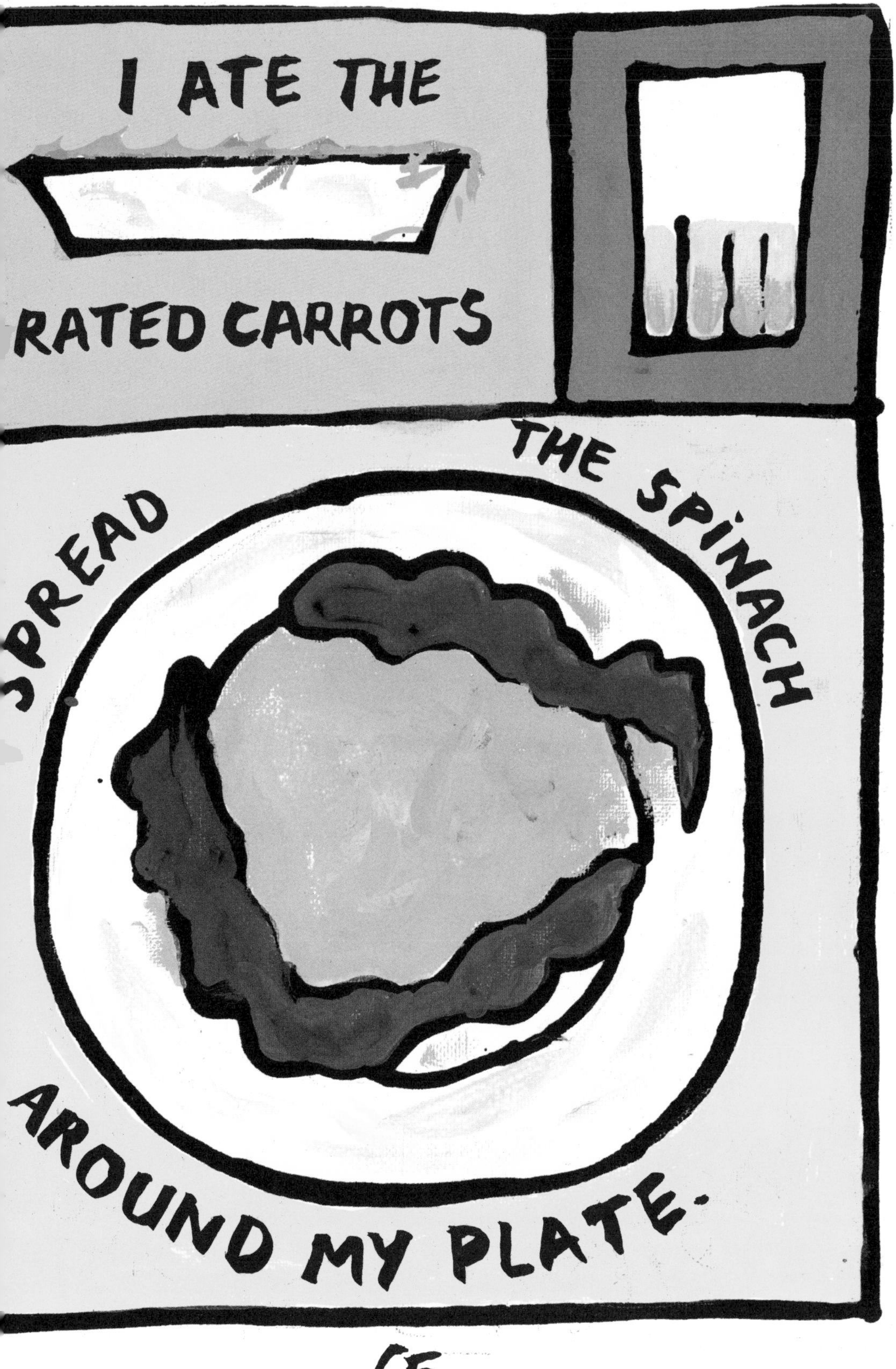
I ATE THE
RATED CARROTS
SPREAD THE SPINACH
AROUND MY PLATE.

"WHAT SMELLS FUNNY?" THE TEACHER ASKED.

OUT OF MY POCKET.

EVERYONE ELSE!

THE END

7

by Adrien and Hélène Riff

Find the seven differences between Adam's father's two class pictures.

ANNÉE SCOLAIRE
1946·1947

ANNÉE SCOLAIRE
1946-1947

Answer
page
81

71

Àt Li'l Marie's school...

by Coralie Gallibour

you can see
the teacher
lose her cool.

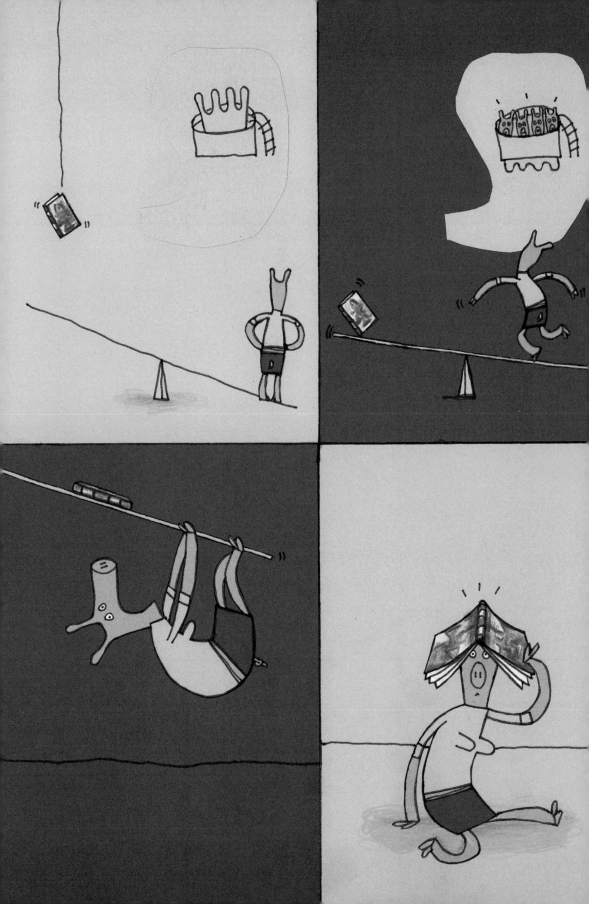

At Li'l Marie's school...
the kids are laughing
in the pool!

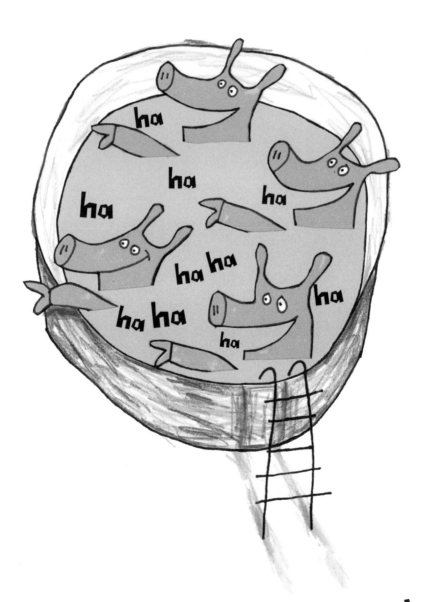

The End